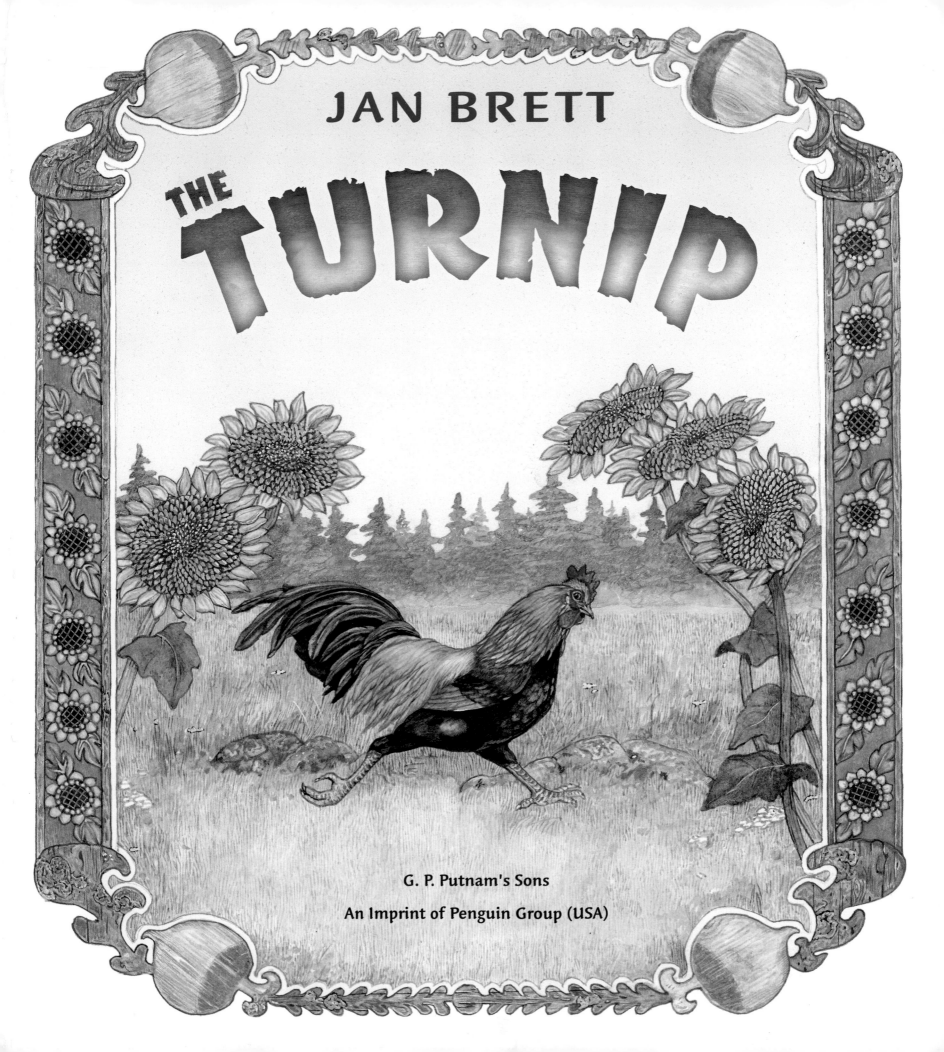

JAN BRETT

THE TURNIP

G. P. Putnam's Sons

An Imprint of Penguin Group (USA)

For Tyler Merrill

G. P. PUTNAM'S SONS
an imprint of Penguin Random House LLC
375 Hudson Street
New York, NY 10014

Library of Congress Cataloging-in-Publication Data
Brett, Jan, 1949– author, illustrator.
The turnip / Jan Brett.
pages cm
Summary: Badger Girl is delighted to find the biggest turnip she has ever seen growing in her vegetable garden,
but when the time comes to harvest the giant root, she is unable to pull it up without help from family and friends.
[1. Turnips—Fiction. 2. Animals—Fiction.] I. Title. PZ7.B7559Tur 2015 [E]—dc23 2015000708

Manufactured in China by RR Donnelley Asia Printing Solutions Ltd.
ISBN 978-0-399-17070-6
1 3 5 7 9 10 8 6 4 2

Design by Marikka Tamura.
Text set in Linotype Syntax Letter Com.
The art for this book was done in watercolors and gouache.
Airbrush backgrounds by Joseph Hearne.

Badger Girl was weeding the vegetable patch when she saw something strange growing in the garden.

It was the biggest turnip she had ever seen.

"Turnip soup, turnip pie," Badger Girl said. "How delicious."

One autumn morning, the air turned chilly. It was time to pick the vegetables and pull up the giant turnip.

But when Badger Girl got to the giant turnip,
she could not pull it up.

"Let me help," Badger Boy offered. "Hang on to me and my strong arms will pull it right out."

They tugged and tugged, but the turnip stayed in place.

"Children," Mother Badger called. "I can wrench that turnip out with a twist and a snap! Watch and learn."

But the turnip remained firmly rooted.

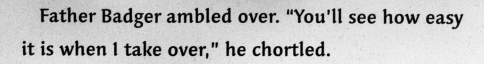

Father Badger ambled over. "You'll see how easy
it is when I take over," he chortled.

Nothing happened.

A snowflake fell from the sky, then another and another.

Once the earth froze, they wouldn't get the turnip
out until spring.

Hedgie was fond of roast turnip. "I know what to do," he said. "I'll stick my prickles into the turnip. We'll all hold hands and give it the heave-ho!"

But the turnip didn't heave or ho.

Mr. Ram, on his way back to town, smiled smugly.
"You country bumpkins don't have the right equipment.
I'll hook it with my horns."

Pull, *pull*, pull! The turnip didn't budge.

Vanya, the horse, stopped by. "I am mighty strong,"
he whinnied. "Hitch my harness to that tasty turnip . . .

. . . and we'll be eating it mashed and salted before it gets dark."

The harness jangled, but when all was settled, the giant turnip was still in the ground.

A cocky little rooster had been watching all along.
He had just had a close call with a cooking pot and
was looking for a new place to live.

Rooster strutted over. "Make room," he crowed.
He took the turnip top in his beak and pulled.

Down in their winter den, the bears found
the giant turnip in their bed.
"Up, up and away!" they shouted.

The turnip flew out of the ground with
Rooster riding high.

"Time for turnip pancakes browned in butter for all,"
Mother Badger sang out . . .

. . . waving her frying pan.

Badger Girl put out their best yellow chair
for Rooster.

Soon the sizzling, crispy turnip pancakes
were ready.

"Rooster, you are invited to stay with us as long as you wish!" Father Badger announced. "After all, when would we ever meet such a useful fellow again?"